dOes a giraffe eVer feel small?

Written by Madeleine Dodge
Illustrated by Olivia Wischmeyer

Axel and Thor —
Stand tall!

Axel & Thor!

ISBN: 0692829837
ISBN-13: 978-0692829837

http://doesagiraffeeverfeelsmall.weebly.com/

Forward

Does a Giraffe Ever Feel Small is a book
for any person who has forgotten their worth.
In this story, the animals of the savanna
overcome their doubts by embracing
the gifts they already hold.

All proceeds made from this book
go toward funding literacy education
with Reading Partners Colorado and Books for Africa.
By sharing this story, we hope to encourage
young people everywhere, to discover and embrace
what makes them unique.

A heartfelt thank you to all of the many people
who believed in us and generously supported this ambition
with donations, professional advice and moral support.
Your encouragement made this book possible.

M.D. and O.W.

To those who read, to those who listen,
and to those who will never stop doing both.

Does a giraffe ever feel small,
like a teeny, tiny ant?

Is she ever discouraged,
or believes that she can't?

Will she ever sit and sulk
because of mean words or jeers?

And when bullies come 'round,
does she cover her ears?

Does a lion ever cower
when the lights go out?

Will he hide from the shadows
with tears on his snout?

Will loud noises make him shake
and hide under the bed?

And will he sniffle and cry
his heart filled with dread?

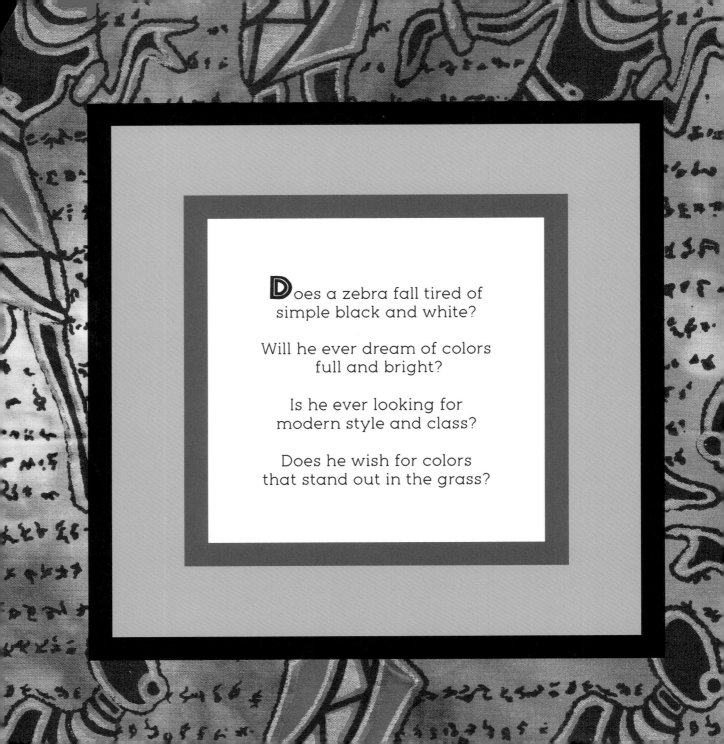

Does a zebra fall tired of
simple black and white?

Will he ever dream of colors
full and bright?

Is he ever looking for
modern style and class?

Does he wish for colors
that stand out in the grass?

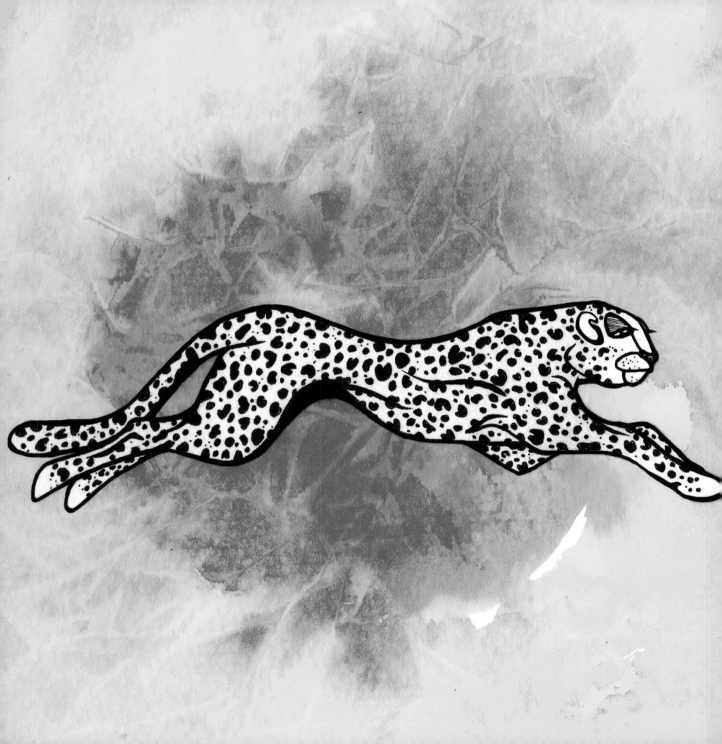

Does a cheetah wish to slow
from her speedy sprint?

Will she ever sit quietly
and watch the sunset glint?

Does she become tired
of the landscape whizzing past?

And is she eager for a turtle's
slow pace at last?

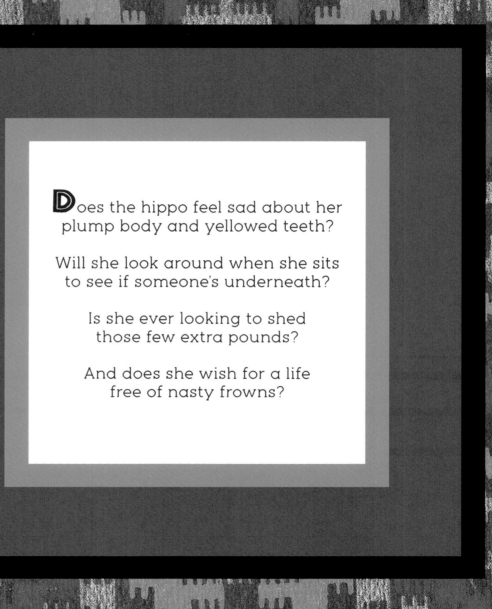

Does the hippo feel sad about her
plump body and yellowed teeth?

Will she look around when she sits
to see if someone's underneath?

Is she ever looking to shed
those few extra pounds?

And does she wish for a life
free of nasty frowns?

Does the itty, bitty fly
feel like he's forgotten?

Is he tired of seeming
so dirty and rotten?

When he cleans up the mess,
does he frown and mutter?

Will he wish to be free
of all the clutter?

no.

Flies are happy
to keep it tidy,

That's their job,
small, but mighty.

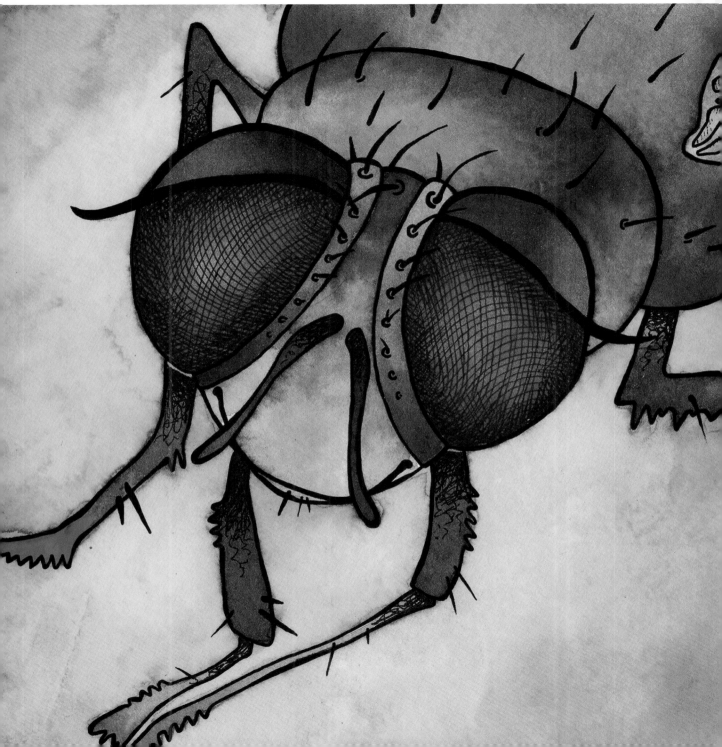

Hippos don't fret
over what they weigh.

Happy in the water,
they splash all day.

Cheetahs can run
without growing weary.

Their journeys and travels
are never dreary.

Zebras love being
black and white.

They don't need color
to feel alright.

Lions know what to do
when they're fearful.

They look to the things
that makes them cheerful.

A giraffe is proud
to be taller than most.

She loves to have
the sky so close.

When swaying high
up in the trees,

She feels happiness, joy,
and most, at ease.

Now learn a lesson
from these animals my friend.

You are different from others,
do not try to pretend

You are unique,
and one of a kind.

Your insides and outsides,
your body and mind.

Whenever you feel
like you might want to fall,

Just simply ask yourself,

"Does a giraffe ever feel small?"

About the Author and Illustrator

Madeleine and Olivia have grown up together, watching the world
through their fiery imaginations and complementing each other
in the best ways. The dream of publishing a book is only one
of the many things they hope to accomplish together.

Meet the Author:

MADELEINE DODGE

Madeleine Dodge is an
avid reader, writer, and dreamer.
Her biggest wish is for a world where
everyone is able to learn freely,
love boundlessly, and live fiercely.

madeleinedodge.weebly.com

Meet the Illustrator:

OLIVIA WISCHMEYER

Olivia Wischmeyer is an artist and
social activist. She believes in the power of
visual messaging and strives to use art as
a tool to bring awareness and change
to the pressing issues of today.

oliviawischmeyerart.weebly.com